The Aristocats

Narinder Dhami

PUFFIN BOOKS

Other titles in the
Disney Classics series:

THE JUNGLE BOOK
LADY AND THE TRAMP
THE LION KING

PUFFIN BOOKS
Published by the Penguin Group: London, New York, Australia, Canada, India New
Zealand and South Africa
Penguin Books Ltd, Registered Offices: 80 Strand, London WC2R 0RL, England

www.penguin.com

First published 2003
1
Copyright © Disney Enterprises, Inc., 2003
All rights reserved
Made and printed in England by Clays Ltd, St Ives plc
ISBN 0–141–31647–0

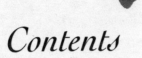

Contents

Chapter One

A large, elegant carriage was driving through the streets of Paris. The horse pulling it wore a hat and sitting astride it was a little ginger kitten. Climbing playfully all over the driver was an equally small, fluffy grey one.

Inside the carriage sat Madame Adelaide Bonfamille. She was petting and stroking a white kitten wearing a pink bow around her neck. 'Marie,' she said, smiling, 'you're going to be as beautiful as your mother.' She turned to the white cat in a jewelled collar who sat beside her. 'Isn't she, Duchess?'

'Meow,' replied Duchess proudly.

Meanwhile, Edgar the driver was trying to shake the kitten off. He frowned crossly and twitched his nose.

'Careful, Toulouse,' Duchess cried. 'You're making it very difficult to drive.'

Edgar let go of the reins, grabbed Toulouse by the scruff of his neck and placed him on the ground just as they reached Madame's home – a big, beautiful house right in the centre of Paris.

'Whoa, Frou-Frou!' the driver said with a scowl.

The horse came to a halt, with Berlioz still clinging to her hat. Edgar climbed down from the carriage and held out his hand to help Madame.

'Thank you, Edgar,' she said. She began to walk towards the house, but then turned back. 'Of course, Frou-Frou! I almost forgot!' She held out a sugar lump to the horse.

Meanwhile, Duchess hurried over to Berlioz and Toulouse. The two kittens were playing around Frou-Frou's legs while the horse stood there patiently.

'Come along, Duchess, kittens,' called

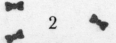

Madame. Edgar was holding the front door open for them. 'Oh, Edgar, I'm expecting my lawyer, George Hautecouer, today. You remember him, of course?'

'Of course, Madame.' Edgar was trying not to sound too grumpy.

Duchess followed Madame up the long, curved staircase to her bedroom, with the three kittens scampering behind them. Madame sat at her dressing table and tidied her hair, while Duchess sat beside her, swinging her fluffy white tail. Meanwhile, the kittens chased each other around the room and played hide-and-seek.

'There now, Duchess, that's better.' Madame tilted her head and stared at her reflection. 'We must both look our best for George.' She reached out and stroked the cat's head. There was a knock at the door.

'Come in,' called Madame.

Edgar stumbled in, breathing hard. 'Announcing Monsieur George Hautecouer,' he panted.

A very old man bounced into the room past Edgar, beaming all over his face. 'Adelaide, my dear,' he said cheerfully, as all the kittens rushed across the room to greet him.

'Good morning, George,' said Madame. 'I hope you're well. I've asked you to come here on a very important legal matter.'

'Oh, splendid!' Monsieur Hautecouer looked at her eagerly. 'Who do you want me to sue?'

'George,' Madame said, 'I simply want to make my will.'

Monsieur Hautecouer lowered himself into a chair with some difficulty. He put on his glasses and picked up a pen. 'So,' he said importantly, 'who are the beneficiaries?'

'Well, as you know, I have no living relatives,' Madame began.

Downstairs in the kitchen, Edgar was doing the ironing. He was also listening to everything that was going on upstairs through a speaking tube on the wall. Madame had one in her bedroom so that

she could call down to the kitchen to tell
Edgar when she was ready for her breakfast
every morning. This meant that Edgar could
hear the conversation taking place above.

'Naturally I want my beloved cats to be
well cared for after I am gone,' Madame
was saying, 'and certainly no one can do
this better than my faithful butler, Edgar.'

Edgar pricked up his ears when he heard
his name. He dashed over to the speaking
tube and listened hard.

'Edgar?' Monsieur Hautecouer sounded
very surprised. 'Adelaide, do you mean to
say that you're leaving your vast fortune to
Edgar?'

The butler's eyes lit up.

'Everything you own?' Monsieur
Hautecouer went on. 'Your money? This
mansion? Your country château?'

Edgar danced a gleeful jig around the
kitchen.

'Your art treasures, your jewels and –'

'No, George, no,' Madame broke in. 'To

my cats.'

Edgar stopped dancing. His shoulders slumped in disappointment and he stared furiously at the speaking tube.

'To your cats?' Monsieur Hautecouer repeated, surprised.

'Yes,' Madame said firmly. 'I wish my cats to inherit first. Then, at the end of their life span, my entire estate will go to Edgar.'

Edgar began to look even angrier as he realized what Madame was saying. 'The cats inherit first and I come next,' he muttered. 'It's not fair! All that money ...'

Suddenly he smiled to himself. Then he began to chuckle. 'There's only one thing for it,' he declared. 'Those cats have got to go!'

Chapter Two

'Me first!'

'No, me first!'

Marie, Toulouse and Berlioz were fighting to get through the cat flap. They all dived for it at exactly the same moment and got stuck.

'Why should you be first?' Toulouse mewed crossly at Marie, as they struggled to get free.

'Because I'm a lady, that's why,' Marie retorted, jumping through the flap.

'You're not a lady,' Toulouse snapped.

'You're nothing but a sister,' Berlioz added.

The three kittens ran into the drawing room and began to chase each other around the furniture.

'I'll show you if I'm a lady or not,' Marie yelled, and she pounced on Berlioz and began pulling at the ribbon round his neck.

'Fight fair, Marie,' Berlioz grumbled.

'Females never fight fair,' said Toulouse, who had climbed on the table to watch. He jumped up on to the big candlestick and knocked the candle down on to Marie's head.

'Ouch,' Marie whimpered. 'That hurt! Mama! *Mama!*'

Duchess padded quickly into the room. 'Marie, darling,' she said softly, 'this is really not ladylike. And, Berlioz –' she turned to stare reproachfully at the other kitten – 'such behaviour is most unbecoming for a gentleman.'

'Well, she started it,' Berlioz muttered. 'We were just practising biting and clawing.'

Duchess looked horrified. 'Aristocats do *not* practise biting and clawing,' she said firmly.

'But some day we might meet a tough

alley cat,' Toulouse chimed in. He jumped down to the floor and strutted around, pretending to be tough. 'MEOW!'

His mother laughed. 'Now that will do,' she said. 'You want to grow up to be charming ladies and gentlemen, don't you? Toulouse, go and start your painting.'

'Mama, can we watch Toulouse paint before our music lesson?' Marie asked.

Duchess nodded and they all gathered round the easel as Toulouse squeezed a big lump of paint out of a tube and started his picture.

'It's Edgar!' Berlioz suddenly burst out, staring at the easel. 'Old Pickle Puss Edgar!'

Duchess tried not to smile. 'Now, now, Berlioz,' she said. 'That's not very kind. You know Edgar is so fond of us ...'

Down in the kitchen, Edgar was humming away happily to himself as he prepared the cats' milk. He bent over the pan that was heating on the stove and dropped some tablets into it. 'Rock-a-bye, kitties, bye-bye you go,' he sang. 'La, la, la, la and I'm in the dough!'

He added some seasoning and then scooped up a little of the warm milk to taste it. He stopped himself just in time.

'Whoops! Oh dear,' he chuckled. 'A slip of the hand and it's off to dreamland!'

Upstairs, Marie and Berlioz had started their piano lessons. They were practising their scales and arpeggios when the door opened. Edgar came in, carrying a tray.

'Ah, good evening, my little ones,' he cried, beaming. He then set down the tray and watched the kittens as they crowded round and began to lap up the milk. 'Sleep well! I – er – I mean, eat well, of course.' Grinning to himself, he left the room.

Duchess joined her kittens and started to drink.

All this time, someone else had been watching the cats. A little mouse was standing shyly next to a hole in the wall, staring at the milk rather hungrily.

The mouse cleared his throat. 'Good evening, Duchess,' he squeaked. 'Hello, kittens.'

'Hello, Roquefort,' the kittens chorused.

'Good evening, Monsieur Roquefort,' said Duchess politely.

'Ummm.' Roquefort sniffed the air. 'Something smells awfully good. What is it?'

'It's crème de la crème à la Edgar,' Marie told him.

'Oh, won't you join us, Monsieur Roquefort?' Duchess asked.

'Well, ah, yes.' Roquefort looked delighted. 'I do happen to have a cracker with me.' And he produced a large biscuit that he had been holding behind his back.

'Come on, Roquefort,' said Berlioz. 'Have some.'

'Oh, thank you.' The mouse scampered over to join them. He dunked his cracker into the milk and took a large bite. 'Very good.'

'This is yummy,' Marie declared.

Roquefort finished his biscuit. 'This calls for another cracker,' he said. 'I'll be right back.'

Berlioz yawned widely as Roquefort scurried off. The mouse was yawning too as he went into his hole. 'So that's crème de la crème à la Edgar,' he murmured drowsily, and immediately fell into a deep, deep sleep.

Chapter Three

It was the middle of the night. Suddenly the
cat flap swung open and a head looked out.
It peered up and down the street, checking
this way and that. But it wasn't a cat. It was
Edgar.

A moment later the door opened and
Edgar tiptoed out, carrying a large basket
with a lid. He tripped over the dustbin and
held his breath for a moment, looking
frightened, but no one came. Chuckling to
himself, he headed over to his motorbike.
He put the basket into the sidecar, then he
lifted the lid and peeped inside. Duchess
and her kittens were curled up together in a
big, fluffy heap, fast asleep. Toulouse opened
her eyes a little but closed them again as
Edgar quickly shut the lid.

Edgar climbed on to the motorbike, revved the engine and set off through the empty streets of Paris. He kept going until he'd left the city far behind and was out in the dark countryside. In the moonlight he could see a windmill ahead of him and he rode towards it.

Beside the windmill was a cart with a dog fast asleep underneath it. He was woken up by an ever-growing rattle coming towards him. The dog lifted his head and listened carefully. Then he jumped to his feet and moved over to the haystack.

'Lafayette!' he barked. 'Hey, Lafayette!'

Another dog's head appeared out of the hay. He was yawning and looked very grumpy. 'I'm right here,' he grumbled.

'Listen.' Napoleon pricked up his ears. 'Wheels approaching.'

'Oh, Napoleon,' Lafayette whined, climbing out of the haystack. 'We bit six tyres today, chased four motorcars and a bicycle *and* a scooter!'

'Hush, a moment,' Napoleon snapped. He listened again. 'It's a motorbike. Two cylinders. One squeaky wheel. Now –' he turned to Lafayette – 'you go for the tyres and I'll go right to the seat of the problem.'

'How come you always grab the tender part for yourself?' Lafayette muttered.

'Because I outrank you, that's why,' Napoleon retorted. The motorbike was getting closer. 'Now sound the attack!'

Lafayette barked loudly. 'OK, let's charge!'

Edgar was bumping along the country road, daydreaming about what he was going to do when he inherited all of Madame's lovely money. He leapt with fright as two big dogs came racing towards him, barking at the tops of their voices. Clutching the handlebars tightly, he tried to turn the motorbike round, but instead he skidded off down an embankment towards a stream.

The basket fell out of the sidecar and into the water, but Edgar didn't notice. He was too busy trying to get away from the two dogs tearing after him.

Frantically, Edgar rode the motorbike through the water. He managed to get out and up the embankment again, but when he glanced down he saw that the two dogs had somehow wedged themselves into his sidecar. They were sitting there, glaring at him.

'Help!' Edgar yelled. He jumped up on to the handlebars as the motorbike careered forward. 'Help!'

Napoleon leaned over and bit the seat of Edgar's trousers. Edgar yelled again, even more loudly. He began hitting Napoleon with his rolled-up umbrella. Suddenly the motorbike hit a tree and split in two: the motorbike went one way and the sidecar another. Edgar rode off quickly, leaving his hat and umbrella behind, as well as the sidecar with Napoleon and Lafayette still inside it.

Meanwhile, Duchess woke up and opened her eyes. For a moment she felt very confused. She was cold and wet, and it was dark.

'Oh, where am I?' Duchess meowed anxiously, looking around. She wasn't at home with Madame in Paris at all. She was lying on the bank of a river, out in the countryside. Then she remembered Berlioz, Toulouse and Marie. 'Children, where are you?' she called at the top of her voice. 'Answer me!'

'Here I am, Mama,' answered Marie. She sounded very frightened.

Duchess looked up to see the little white kitten caught in a tree. She hurried over and took her down gently. 'Marie, darling, are you all right?'

'I guess I had a nightmare and fell out of bed,' Marie replied, cuddling close to her mother.

'Mama! Mama!'

'That's Berlioz,' said Marie, staring around with wide eyes.

Looking very sorry for himself, a wet and shivering Berlioz climbed out of the stream. 'Ooh, I'm cold, Mama,' he whimpered.

'*Croak!*' said a frog sitting on the river bank.

Berlioz nearly jumped out of his skin. 'Mama!' he yelled. He raced over to Duchess and crouched down between her legs.

Duchess laughed. 'Darling, that's only a little frog,' she explained.

'But he had a mouth like a hipolatamus!' gasped Berlioz.

The frog laughed and so did Marie.

Berlioz glared at her. 'Hey, what's so funny?'

'Now, now, darlings,' Duchess said soothingly. 'You just stay here while I look for Toulouse.' She glanced around. 'Toulouse, where are you?'

Toulouse popped his head out of the basket. 'What's all the yelling about?' he asked.

'Oh, thank goodness.' Duchess hurried

over to him. 'Are you all right?'

'I was having a funny dream.' Toulouse yawned as his mother licked his face. 'Edgar was in it.'

The frog croaked again loudly.

'Oh,' Toulouse gasped. 'It *wasn't* a dream. Edgar did this to us!'

'That's ridiculous, darling,' Duchess said gently.

A large clap of thunder overhead made them all jump.

'Mama, I want to go home,' Marie mewed.

'Quickly, let's get into the basket,' said Duchess, as the rain began to pour down.

So they all climbed in and snuggled down.

'What's going to happen to us?' Toulouse wanted to know.

'I wish we were home with Madame right now,' said Berlioz sadly.

'Poor Madame,' Duchess sighed. 'She'll be so worried when she finds us missing ...'

Chapter Four

'Oh! Duchess! Kittens!' Madame sat up in bed, looking pale and worried. It was the middle of the night and outside the big old house the storm was raging. 'I had the most horrible dream about you.' She slipped out of bed and put on her robe and slippers. 'Thank goodness it *was* only a dream. Oh dear, what a terrible night.'

Madame hurried over to the cat bed by the window. 'Now, now, my darlings,' she began, pulling back the blanket. 'Don't be frightened.'

But the bed was empty.

'Oh no!' Madame gasped in horror. 'They're gone!'

She rushed over to the bedroom door, flung it open and ran down the hall, calling,

'Duchess! Kittens! Where are you? Where have you gone?'

The noise woke up Roquefort, who was still sleeping peacefully in his mouse-hole. He rushed out and jumped up on to the banister. 'Duchess and the kittens gone?' he said anxiously. 'Why, that's terrible!'

Roquefort peered out of the window. The rain was streaming down and every so often there was a flash of lightning, followed by a loud clap of thunder.

'Good heavens, anything could happen to them on a night like this,' he muttered. He ran back to his hole, put on his hat and coat, and then hurried downstairs to the cat flap.

'I've just got to find them,' he said to himself as he climbed through. 'Duchess!' The little mouse rushed down the street, looking in every dark corner. 'Kittens!'

But there was no sign of them anywhere ...

When morning came the storm had cleared, the sky was blue and the sun was shining.

The three kittens were still sleeping peacefully in the basket, while Duchess was curled up on the grass.

Suddenly she opened her eyes. What was that noise? Someone was singing – and it was coming closer.

'I'm Abraham de Lacy Giuseppe Casey Thomas O'Malley, the alley cat!'

A big, battered-looking ginger tom was padding along the bank of the stream towards Duchess. When he spotted the pretty white cat staring at him, he grinned, jumped up into a tree and shook some flower petals down on to her. Duchess pretended not to notice and calmly began to lick her paw.

'Whatever I take is the road I make,' O'Malley continued to sing lazily. 'It's the road of life, make no mistake, for me. Abraham de Lacy Giuseppe Casey Thomas O'Malley, the alley cat!'

'Bravo!' Duchess cried. 'You have a great talent.'

'Thank you,' O'Malley purred. 'And what might *your* name be?'

'Duchess,' she told him.

'Beautiful,' O'Malley purred. 'I love it. Your blue eyes are like sapphires sparkling so bright!'

'Very poetic,' replied Duchess. 'But, you see, Monsieur O'Malley, I'm really in a great deal of trouble.'

'Trouble?' O'Malley jumped down from the tree and sprawled at Duchess's feet. 'Now, what's the problem, Your Ladyship?'

'Well, it's most important that I get back to Paris,' Duchess replied. 'So if you could just show me the way –'

'We shall fly to Paris on a magic carpet!' O'Malley purred, moving closer to her. 'Just us two.'

'That sounds wonderful!' mewed Marie, climbing out of the basket.

O'Malley jumped and looked round. His face dropped when he saw Marie. 'Three?' he spluttered.

Berlioz and Toulouse hurried to join their sister.

'Four?' O'Malley stammered. 'Five?'

'Oh yes, Monsieur,' Duchess said sweetly. 'These are my children.'

Berlioz bounced over to O'Malley. 'Do you really have a magic carpet?' he asked eagerly.

'And are we going to ride on it?' Marie added.

O'Malley looked very embarrassed. 'Well – er –'

Duchess sighed. 'I understand perfectly, Monsieur O'Malley,' she said. 'Well, come along, children.'

O'Malley watched them set off along the river bank. 'Hey, hold on there,' he called, running after Duchess and the kittens.

Duchess turned round. 'Yes, Monsieur O'Malley?'

'Now look, kids.' O'Malley stared down at the kittens. 'If I said magic carpet, that's what it's going to be. And it's going to stop

for us right here!' He drew a line in the
ground with his claw, as the kittens
watched. 'Now you just hide over there.'

The kittens hurried Duchess into a clump
of bushes while O'Malley climbed up a
nearby tree.

'Quick, Mama,' Toulouse said urgently.

'But, children –' Duchess began
anxiously. She wasn't at all sure whether
this tough alley cat was really going to help
them or not.

'Hurry, Mama,' Berlioz told her.

As O'Malley peered down the road, he
saw a milk truck heading towards them.
'One magic carpet coming up,' he
announced. Crouching down in the tree, he
waited until the truck drew level. Then he
jumped down and landed on the bonnet
with a bloodcurdling screech.

'MEOWWWW!'

'*Sacre bleu!*' yelled the milkman, who was
nearly frightened out of his wits.

The milk truck swerved across the road

and came to an abrupt stop. The driver got out to see where the cat had gone, but O'Malley had sneaked round the back and was calling to Duchess and the kittens.

'All aboard for Paris!' he mewed, helping them to climb up among the milk churns.

'How can we ever thank you?' Duchess asked, looking down at the alley cat standing in the road.

'My pleasure entirely,' O'Malley called as the truck began to move off again.

Marie leaned out to wave at him. Then: 'OH!' she gasped as she tumbled forward, landing in the road as the others sped off.

'Marie!' Duchess called, her eyes wide with horror.

O'Malley swept forward, scooped Marie up in his mouth and chased after them. He managed to grab the back of the truck, clinging on with his claws, and handed Marie to her mother. Then he climbed up to join them.

'Thank you for saving my life, Monsieur

O'Malley,' Marie said gratefully.

'No trouble at all, little princess,' O'Malley replied. He looked round at the three kittens. 'And when we get to Paris, I'll show you the time of your lives!'

'Oh, I'm so sorry,' Duchess broke in, 'but we can't. You see, we must go straight home. My mistress will be so worried about us.'

O'Malley looked surprised. 'Well, humans don't really worry too much about their pets,' he said.

'Oh no.' Duchess shook her head. 'You just don't understand. She loves us very much. Poor Madame!'

Roquefort trudged slowly into the coach house. Frou-Frou, who was in her stall, looked anxiously at him.

'Oh, Roquefort, I've been so worried about you,' she neighed. 'Did you have any luck?'

Roquefort shook his head. 'Not a sign of them, Frou-Frou,' he said sadly. 'I've searched all night.'

'And poor Madame didn't sleep a wink either,' added Frou-Frou.

'Oh, it's a sad day for all of us,' Roquefort sighed.

'La la la la la!'

Roquefort and Frou-Frou stared at each other in surprise as they heard the sound of cheerful singing from outside the coach house. The next moment, Edgar bounced in, swinging a pail of oats.

'Morning, Frou-Frou!' he said jauntily. 'Can you keep a secret? Of course you can!' He pulled a newspaper from under his arm and shook it out. 'Look, Frou-Frou, I've made the headlines!'

Roquefort scrambled up on to the horse's head to take a look. The headline on the front page read, 'Mysterious Catnapper Abducts Family of Cats'.

Edgar laughed. 'Aren't you proud of me?' he crowed.

'So *he's* the catnapper,' Roquefort

'We must look our best for Monsieur Hautecouer!'

'I leave my fortune to my cats.' Madame's voice floated down the speaking tube.

'Rock-a-bye, kitties, bye-bye you go!'

The basket fell out of the sidecar and into the water, but Edgar didn't notice.

'I'm Abraham DeLacy Giuseppe Casey Thomas O'Malley, the alley cat!'

'I know a place where we can stay – my own penthouse pad!'

'*Everybody wants to be a cat,*' sang Scat Cat.

'Hurrah, we're home!' mewed Toulouse, and the kittens ran toward the house.

'Look out for the sack!' Roquefort yelled.

Now, my pesky little pets, you're going to travel first class!' Edgar said.

'Over there!' O'Malley yelled. 'They're in the trunk!'

Frou-Frou kicked out and Edgar landed in the trunk with a thump

'Now, don't move. Say cheese!' Madame laughed.

whispered in Frou-Frou's ear.

'The police said it was a professional, masterful job,' Edgar went on smugly. 'Not bad, eh, Frou-Frou, old girl?'

He tapped Frou-Frou on the back with the newspaper. The horse jumped and tossed Roquefort off her head. The mouse landed right in the middle of Frou-Frou's dinner.

'That sneaky, no-good butler,' Roquefort mumbled, spitting out a mouthful of oats.

'Oh, they won't find any clues,' Edgar chuckled. 'Not a single one.' But suddenly his face turned pale. 'Oh! My hat! My umbrella!' The butler had just remembered that he'd left them at the scene of the crime. 'Oh, gracious,' he moaned. 'I've got to get those things back – tonight!'

Chapter Five

'Anyone for breakfast?'

Thomas O'Malley pulled away the cover on the back of the milk truck to reveal a churn labelled 'Cream'.

'Hurrah!' Marie cheered.

'Look, Mama, look,' said Toulouse excitedly.

The three kittens jumped on to the churn and began lapping up their breakfast.

'Why, Monsieur O'Malley,' Duchess said, laughing, 'you are quite amazing.'

'True,' O'Malley purred.

Unfortunately, just at that moment the driver happened to glance in his rear-view mirror. He saw the kittens drinking his cream and his mouth fell open in amazement.

'*Sacre bleu!*' he roared, and jammed the brakes on.

O'Malley was tossed up into the air and he landed smack on the driver's head. Both the driver and O'Malley let out a loud screech, but the alley cat escaped by leaping from the window. Meanwhile, Duchess was helping the kittens to jump off the back of the truck.

'Thieves!' the driver yelled, shaking his fist at them as they ran across the railway tracks. 'Robbers!'

O'Malley led them into a tool shed at the side of the railway line. They peered out to see if the angry man was following them, but he had driven off.

'Oh, what a horrible, horrible human,' Duchess gasped. 'I'll be so glad when we get back home.'

'That's a long way away, so we'd better get moving,' replied O'Malley.

They set off again, walking along the side of the railway track, the kittens bounding along in front. The track led them to a bridge that spanned a wide stream.

'Let's play trains,' Toulouse suggested.

'All aboard,' Berlioz shouted.

'Now, children, be careful,' Duchess warned them as Marie joined in.

'Choo-choo!' yelled Toulouse as the three kittens ran along the railway line. Suddenly there was a loud whistle. A train was rumbling down the track towards them and it was going very fast.

'Oh no!' Duchess gasped.

'Quick!' O'Malley sprang forward. 'Get underneath here.'

The cats huddled together under a plank at the side of the track as the train wheels roared past them. The ground shook and the noise was deafening, but they were all safe.

Then suddenly there was a loud splash.

'Mama!' Marie cried. She had fallen off the bridge into the water below.

'Marie!' Duchess was horrified as she stared down at the struggling kitten.

Marie was trying to swim, but she kept sinking.

'Keep your head up, Marie,' O'Malley shouted. 'Here I come.'

With that he dived into the water, scooped Marie up in his mouth and grabbed on to a log that was floating down the stream.

Duchess ran along the branch of a tree that hung over the water. 'Thomas,' she called. 'Up here!'

As O'Malley drifted past, he flipped Marie up into the air towards her mother. Duchess caught her safely. She put her down with Toulouse and Berlioz, then rushed back to see what had happened to O'Malley. He was being pulled along by the strong current.

'Take care, Thomas,' Duchess called anxiously.

'I'm all right,' O'Malley spluttered, still clinging to the log. 'I'll see you further downstream.' And he floated on.

Chapter Six

Duchess and the kittens were running along the river bank, trying to find O'Malley. Duchess felt very worried about him. He had tried to help them and so far they had been nothing but trouble.

'Look, Ma,' Berlioz mewed. 'There he is.'

Two geese were carrying O'Malley out of the water towards the bank. The alley cat was soaking wet and looked half drowned.

'Can I help you, Monsieur O'Malley?' Toulouse called.

'I've had all the help I can take,' O'Malley spluttered, glaring at the geese.

Duchess rushed over to him. 'Oh, Thomas, thank goodness you're safe.' She turned to the geese. 'Thank you so much for saving Monsieur O'Malley.'

'I'm Amelia Gabble and this is my sister, Abigail,' Amelia said, beaming. 'We're on holiday.'

'A walking tour of France,' Abigail added.

'This is Thomas O'Malley, who is a dear friend of ours,' Duchess explained. 'He's helping us to get to Paris.'

'Well, girls, see you around,' O'Malley broke in hastily. 'Come on, Duchess, time to split.'

'Frou-Frou, here comes Edgar!'

Roquefort was peering out of the coach-house window. He turned and jumped on to the horse, ran up her nose and down her back, and slid down her tail to the ground.

'Hurry, Roquefort,' Frou-Frou neighed.

'Hop on to the motorbike and for goodness sake be careful.'

Edgar hurried into the coach house carrying a fishing rod. He went over to his motorbike, which was parked next to Frou-Frou's stall. 'Tonight Operation Catnapper will be completed, Frou-Frou,' he told the horse.

He then climbed on to his battered motorbike, put on his goggles and revved up the engine. Roquefort almost fell out of the broken tail-light as they sped off, but he managed to hold on and wave to Frou-Frou.

Edgar raced through the empty city streets as fast as he could. Poor Roquefort was bumped and banged from side to side. Suddenly he was tossed through the air and landed with a thump on the ground. Edgar and the motorbike were gone in a flash.

Picking himself up, Roquefort felt utterly miserable. He'd never find out what had happened to Duchess and the kittens now ...

Edgar travelled far out into the countryside, towards the windmill where he'd been attacked by the two dogs. This time he parked the motorbike a little way away. Then he took the fishing rod and tiptoed towards the cart. He peered underneath it,

but there were no dogs there, so he went
towards the haystack. He looked round it
and saw Napoleon and Lafayette asleep.
Napoleon was in the sidecar, wearing
Edgar's hat, with the umbrella beside him.
Lafayette was curled up in the cats' basket.

Suddenly Napoleon began to stir. Hastily
Edgar pulled back out of sight.

'Lafayette, listen.' Napoleon sat up.
'Squeaky shoes approaching.'

'That ain't nothing but a little old cricket.'
Lafayette yawned.

Looking alarmed, Edgar took his shoes
off and left them on the ground.

Lafayette yawned again. 'I'll see you in
the morning, Napoleon,' he mumbled, and
went back to asleep.

Edgar waited until Napoleon was asleep
too. Then he climbed up the haystack and
unreeled the fishing line. Carefully, he
dangled the hook beneath the rim of
Napoleon's hat and tried to pull it off the
horse's head, but it didn't catch. After

several unsuccessful attempts at grabbing it he eventually managed to grasp it in his teeth. Then he let down the line again to get the umbrella. But this time he hooked the basket by mistake. Lafayette tumbled out and landed in the sidecar with Napoleon.

'What's going on?' Napoleon spluttered as Edgar quickly hooked up the umbrella and reeled it in. 'Where's my hat? Where's my umbrella?'

Edgar peered over the top of the haystack as the two dogs jumped out of the sidecar and began looking around.

'Listen.' Napoleon's ears pricked up. 'You're not going to believe this – but it's a one-wheeled haystack!'

The dogs stared as the haystack whizzed down the road, travelling along on one wheel. Barking, the two dogs flung themselves at it and disappeared into the pile of hay. Suddenly the hay flew off and landed on top of the cart, taking the two dogs with it. And underneath was Edgar in the sidecar, clutching the basket. He jumped out and on to his motorbike. Using the umbrella to hook the sidecar to the motorbike, he drove off triumphantly.

Chapter Seven

Duchess, Berlioz and Toulouse followed O'Malley, who was carrying Marie on his back, across the rooftops. Not far away, the Eiffel Tower loomed up into the night sky. They had made it back to Paris, and said goodbye to Amelia and Abigail. But they were still quite a way from Madame's house.

Duchess turned to O'Malley. 'Madame will be so worried,' she said anxiously. 'Are you sure we can't get home tonight?'

'It's late and the kids are tired,' O'Malley replied. 'I told you, I know a place where we can stay.' He grinned. 'And there it is – my own penthouse pad!'

They were looking at an attic right at the top of a tumble-down old house. Suddenly the window flew open, the light went on and loud jazz music began to play. The kittens perked up, looking interested.

O'Malley groaned. 'Oh no! Sounds like Scat Cat and his gang!'

'Friends of yours?' enquired Duchess.

'Yeah,' O'Malley replied. 'They're real swingers! But – er – not exactly your type, Duchess.'

'On the contrary.' Duchess shook her head. 'I'd like to meet them.'

The kittens had already run over to look through the open window. A gang of cats was standing around, playing various musical instruments. One sat at a drum kit, while the others were playing saxophone, double bass, guitar and accordion.

'Hey, look,' shouted the biggest cat, who held the saxophone. 'Big man O'Malley is back in his alley!'

'Hey, Scat Cat,' O'Malley called. He swung through the window and landed on the bed. 'Duchess, this is the greatest cat of them all.'

'I'm delighted to meet you.' Duchess
smiled.

'Likewise.' Scat Cat beamed, kissing her
paw.

'Oh, your music is so different,' Duchess
went on. 'So exciting.'

'It isn't Beethoven, Mama,' Berlioz broke
in, his eyes shining, 'but it sure bounces!'

Scat Cat leaned on the piano and grinned
down at the kitten. 'Say, this kitten cat
knows where it's at!' He began to sing.
'Everybody wants to be a cat, because a
cat's the only cat who knows where it's at …'

The band started to play loudly. Berlioz
and Toulouse rushed to the piano to join in,
while Duchess and O'Malley began to
dance together. Marie jumped around on
the floor, singing along with Scat Cat.

'Everybody … everybody … everybody
wants to be a cat!'

The old house was quiet now. Scat Cat and
his gang had gone, and Duchess was

tucking Berlioz, Toulouse and Marie into bed. All three kittens were very sleepy.

'Sweet dreams,' Duchess said, and went to join O'Malley, who was sitting on the window-sill. 'They could hardly keep their eyes open,' she said, laughing.

Marie sat up in bed and peered out of the window. She could hear everything her mother and O'Malley were saying.

'Thomas, thank you very much for bringing us to your home,' Duchess said softly.

O'Malley looked embarrassed. 'Well, it needs a bit of tidying up and, well, maybe –' He cleared his throat.

'A little feminine touch?' Duchess suggested.

O'Malley stared at her. 'Your eyes *are* like sapphires!' he said. 'You know, Duchess, all those little kittens, I love 'em.'

'And they are very fond of you,' Duchess replied.

Berlioz and Toulouse had crept over to join Marie and they were all listening hard.

'They need a – well – a father,' O'Malley said awkwardly.

Marie, Berlioz and Toulouse looked at each other in delight.

'Oh, Thomas, that would be wonderful,' Duchess gasped. But then she shook her head sadly. 'If only I could …'

'But why can't you?' O'Malley asked anxiously.

'Because of Madame,' replied Duchess. 'I could never leave her.'

O'Malley looked puzzled. 'But Madame's only a human. You're just her house pets.'

'Oh no.' Duchess shook her head. 'We mean far more to her than that. I'm sorry, but we must go home tomorrow.'

'Well, I guess you know best,' O'Malley sighed. 'But I'm going to miss you. And those kids.'

'We almost had a father,' Berlioz whimpered to Toulouse and Marie.

'Yeah,' Toulouse agreed sadly. 'Come on. We'd better go back to bed.'

Chapter Eight

'Are you sure we're on the right street?'
O'Malley asked, as Duchess rushed ahead
of him.

It was the following morning. They had
set out early and at last they had almost
reached Madame's house.

'Yes, yes,' Duchess cried excitedly. 'Hurry!'

They ran along the street towards the
house. A mouse was sitting in one of the
windows with his nose pressed dejectedly
against the glass. It was Roquefort.
Suddenly he leapt to his feet, hardly
believing his eyes. A pretty white cat and
three kittens were running towards him.

'It's Duchess!' he squeaked. 'And the
kittens! They're back!'

Beaming all over his face, Roquefort slid

45

down the curtains and raced to the door.
Then he skidded to a halt. Edgar was sitting
in the drawing room, clutching a bottle of
champagne in an ice bucket.

Roquefort went cold all over.

'Oh no! Edgar!' he muttered. 'I've got to
do something, quick.'

'Ho ho ho!' Edgar chuckled. He lifted the
bottle out of the ice bucket and began to
pop the cork. 'Get used to the finer things in
life, old chap,' he said cheerfully, 'because
some day they're all going to be yours!'

Roquefort sidled over to Edgar and
jumped on to his shoe. Quickly and neatly,
he tied the laces together.

'You sly old fox,' Edgar chortled to
himself. At that moment, the cork popped
out of the bottle and hit Roquefort in the
tummy, knocking him against the wall.

'Hurrah, we're home!' mewed Toulouse, as
the kittens ran towards the house.

'Wait for me,' Marie yelled.

All three kittens headed for the cat flap, but they bounced straight off it again.

'It's locked,' Berlioz whimpered.

'Come on,' Marie suggested. 'Let's all meow.'

The three kittens began to mew as loudly as they could.

Inside the house, Edgar took a sip of champagne, but then he blew the whole lot out again in surprise when he heard the noise. 'It *can't* be them,' he muttered.

Roquefort picked himself up and raced to the window. At the same moment, Edgar jumped up and immediately fell right over because his shoelaces were tied together.

'Go away!' Roquefort waved frantically at the kittens through the window. 'Don't come in!'

'Look, there's Roquefort,' Toulouse said cheerfully, waving at the mouse.

'Hi, Roquefort,' Marie called.

'He looks glad to see us,' said Berlioz, watching the mouse jump up and down.

Meanwhile, Duchess and O'Malley were standing together at the gate.

'I don't know what to say,' Duchess murmured sadly. 'I only wish –'

'Maybe just a short goodbye would be easiest,' O'Malley said quickly.

'I'll never forget you, Thomas O'Malley,' Duchess whispered. Then she turned and followed the kittens across the courtyard.

The door was opening. Berlioz, Toulouse and Marie rushed into the kitchen, mewing with delight at being home again. Their mother followed them.

'Don't come in!' Roquefort squeaked from behind the curtain.

But it was too late. The tall, spindly figure of Edgar loomed over them.

'Duchess,' he said in an oily voice, 'wherever have you been?'

'Look out for the sack!' Roquefort yelled,

rushing forward.

Again he was too late. Edgar had already trapped Duchess and the kittens in the sack and scooped them up.

Outside, Thomas O'Malley took one last look at the house and then turned to leave.

'Well, I guess they won't need me any more,' he told himself sadly as he trudged down the street.

Chapter Nine

'You came back,' Edgar complained, tying a knot firmly in the top of the sack. 'It's just not fair!'

'Edgar! Edgar!' Madame was calling from upstairs.

Edgar panicked. He threw the sack into the oven, slammed the door shut and snarled, 'I'll deal with you later!' Then he dashed out of the room.

Madame was hurrying down the steps towards him, looking excited.

'Oh, Edgar, they're back!' she declared. 'I heard them! Hurry! Hurry and let them in.'

Pretending to look pleased, Edgar opened the front door and peered out.

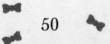

Madame rushed out on to the porch, looking up and down the street. 'Duchess, kittens, where are you?' she called. 'Come here, my darlings.'

Edgar cleared his throat. 'Allow me, Madame,' he said smugly. 'Here, kitty!'

Back in the kitchen, Roquefort raced over to the oven. 'Duchess, it's me,' he whispered. 'What can I do to help?'

'Fetch O'Malley,' Duchess replied. 'And hurry!'

Roquefort jumped down to the floor. 'Yes, yes, I'm on my way!'

'I told you it was Edgar,' Toulouse whimpered inside the sack.

'Oh, shut up!' said Berlioz.

Meanwhile, Madame had returned to the house, looking very sad. 'It's no use, Edgar,' she murmured. 'I'm afraid it was just the imagination of an old lady. But I was so sure I heard them.'

'I'm sorry, Madame,' Edgar smirked.

Roquefort ran down the street after O'Malley. He just caught sight of the tip of the alley cat's tail disappearing round the corner and he chased after him.

'Hey, stop!' Roquefort panted. 'Duchess, kittens – in trouble!' He took a deep breath. 'The butler did it!'

'Duchess and the kittens in trouble?' O'Malley stared at him. 'Look, you go and get Scat Cat and his gang of alley cats –'

Roquefort looked terrified. 'Alley cats?' he squeaked. 'But I'm a mouse!'

'Move!' O'Malley said urgently. 'Just tell 'em O'Malley sent you and you won't have a bit of trouble.' Then he ran back towards Madame's house.

'No trouble, he said,' Roquefort muttered as he scurried across town towards the alley where the cats hung out. 'That's easy for what's-his-name to say. He's got nine lives.'

Suddenly he was picked up by his tail.

Roquefort squawked with fright as he looked into the face of Scat Cat.

'What's a little swinger like you doing on our side of town?' Scat Cat demanded lazily, as the other cats gathered round.

'Oh, please,' Roquefort begged. 'I was sent here for help. By a cat.'

'Crazy!' Scat Cat murmured. He dropped the mouse on the ground and Roquefort scuttled inside a nearby bottle. One of the other cats picked it up and stared at the mouse.

'Honest!' Roquefort squeaked. 'He told me just to say his name.'

The cat hit the bottle and Roquefort flew out and landed in another cat's paws. 'So what's his name?' he asked, peering at the frightened mouse.

Roquefort racked his brains. He just couldn't remember. 'Er – his name is O'Toole,' he said hopefully.

'I don't know that guy,' Scat Cat said. 'Strike one!'

'O'Brien?' Roquefort spluttered.

'Strike two!' announced Scat Cat.

'How about O'Grady?' Roquefort stammered.

'Mousy, you just struck out.' Scat Cat tickled Roquefort under the chin with one of his claws. 'Any last words?'

'Oh, why did I listen to that O'Malley cat?' Roquefort groaned.

Scat Cat's ears immediately pricked up. 'O'Malley? Hey, you guys, this mouse is on the level!'

'Of course I'm on the level!' Roquefort squeaked. 'Duchess and the kittens are in trouble, and O'Malley needs help!'

Scat Cat turned to his gang. 'Come on, cats,' he said. 'We gotta split!'

Chapter Ten

O'Malley peered in through the window. Edgar was on the telephone, holding a sackful of wriggling cats. O'Malley watched him hang up the receiver and then rush out to the coach house. The alley cat followed him.

Frou-Frou looked up as Edgar came in, carrying the sack.

'Now, my pesky little pets,' Edgar muttered, 'you're going to travel first class.' He opened up a large trunk and put the sack inside, then he banged the lid shut. On the top was a label which read 'To Timbuktu, Africa'.

O'Malley edged his way through the coach-house window and up into the loft.

'But we've got to hurry,' Edgar went on.

'The baggage trunk will be here any
moment now.'

Suddenly O'Malley landed right on top of
Edgar, knocking him over. The cat jumped
to his feet and then rushed to push the
coach-house door shut. Muttering crossly,
Edgar tried to chase after him, but Frou-
Frou caught his coat tails in her teeth and
held on tightly.

'Let go!' Edgar pulled his coat free and
began pushing the trunk towards the door.
O'Malley clung on to the other end, trying
to stop him, and Frou-Frou joined in too,
stepping in front of the trunk so that
Edgar's path was blocked.

Grabbing a pitchfork, Edgar chased
O'Malley around the coach house. He
pinned the alley cat against the wall and
rushed over to the door. But when he
opened it, Edgar's eyes almost popped out
of his head as Scat Cat and his gang raced
in with Roquefort.

'Over there!' O'Malley yelled. 'They're in

the trunk!'

Roquefort began trying to undo the lock, as Scat Cat and his gang surrounded Edgar. O'Malley managed to free himself and dashed across to the trunk, just as Roquefort got the lock open.

'Quick!' O'Malley pulled open the sack and grabbed the nearest kitten. 'Everybody get out of here fast!'

Edgar roared with fury as he saw Duchess and the kittens escaping. 'You're going to Timbuktu,' he shouted, 'if it's the last thing I do!'

Two of the cats threw a horse collar around Edgar's neck, pinning his arms to his sides, and Scat Cat threw a bucket of water over him. As Edgar spluttered angrily, one of the cat gang attached him to a pulley. Frou-Frou tugged on the rope and Edgar swung up into the air. The horse kicked out and Edgar sailed across the coach house, landing in the empty trunk with a thump. The lid closed and the trunk slid right out of the door, just as a van drew up outside.

Roquefort, Frou-Frou and the cats peered out of the window as the van driver climbed out.

'Well, this must be the trunk,' he said to his helper.

'And it goes all the way to Timbuktu,' the boy added.

They put the trunk into the back of the van and drove off. Duchess and O'Malley turned to each other and began to laugh.

'A little closer, my pets.' Madame looked through the camera at Duchess, O'Malley and the kittens on the love-seat. 'Good. What do you think, George?'

'Very good,' said Monsieur Hautecouer, who was sitting at the desk. 'But I think we should get on with the will.' He picked up his pen. 'We need to take the butler out.'

'You know, George,' Madame said thoughtfully. 'If Edgar had known about the will, I'm sure he would never have left so suddenly.' She smiled. 'Duchess, it's wonderful to have you all back. And as for this young man –' she stroked O'Malley's head – 'shall we keep him in the family?'

'MEW!' said the kittens eagerly.

'Of course we shall!' Madame laughed. 'We need a man around the house.' She looked through the camera again. 'Now, don't move. Say cheese!'

'Did someone say cheese?' demanded Roquefort, popping out of his hole.

The camera flashed as Madame took the picture. 'Now run along downstairs,' she told the cats. 'There's a surprise for you.'

Roquefort grabbed on to Berlioz's tail and followed the cats downstairs. Monsieur Hautecouer frowned and put down his pen.

'Adelaide, what's that music?' he asked.

'That's the start of my new foundation.' Madame laughed. 'My home for all the alley cats of Paris!'

Downstairs, Duchess, O'Malley and the

kittens stared in delight at Scat Cat and his gang gathered around the piano.

'Everybody wants to be a cat!' Scat Cat sang loudly, grinning at O'Malley and Duchess.

And everybody, including Roquefort and Frou-Frou, joined in the singing.